121 Epic Things
About Junior High

Bigger, Cooler Middle Schooler.
Copyright © 2025 by Bluestone Books.
All rights reserved.
Any unauthorized duplication in whole or in part or dissemination of this edition by any means (including but not limited to photocopying, electronic devices, digital versions, and the internet) will be prosecuted to the fullest extent of the law.

Published by Bluestone Books
www.bluestonebooks.co

Special thanks to Violet and Mila for their expertise and insights.

ISBN 978-1-965636-00-8 (trade paperback)

Printed in China
First Edition: 2025

10 9 8 7 6 5 4 3 2 1

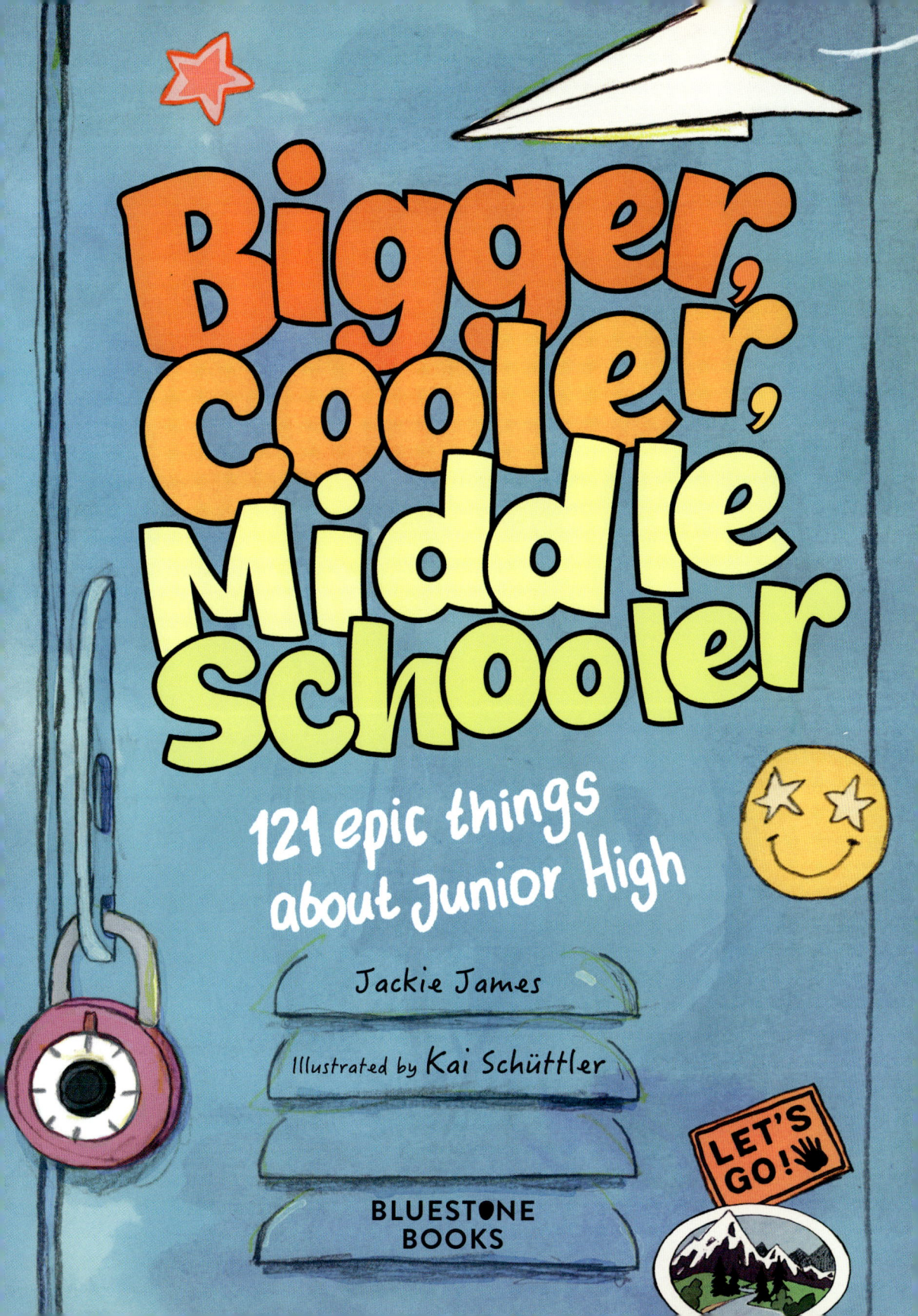

Bigger, Cooler, Middle Schooler

121 epic things about Junior High

Jackie James

Illustrated by Kai Schüttler

BLUESTONE BOOKS

You know how your parents get that weird look on their faces when they talk about middle school, and it makes you a little nervous?

You know how the teachers are all like, "You're gonna love middle school," but they also said that about the 4th grade field trip to the town hall where you were bored out of your mind?

You deserve the real story about middle school from people who have lived it. 8th graders, like us.

The good news is, it definitely will be awesome. Sure, you'll have to adjust to new routines and a bigger school, but YOU'VE GOT THIS.

⋛BEHOLD⋚
121 epic things you'll love about middle school...

 Hallway freedom! (Single-file lines are so last year.)

 Time to chat (or fist-bump) with friends between classes.

 Big fat textbooks that make you look smart carrying them.

 Plus a locker to stash them in so your arms don't fall off.

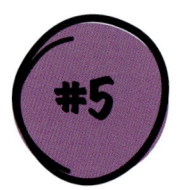

#5 Adventurous teachers.

#6 Science projects where you get to launch stuff!

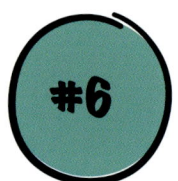

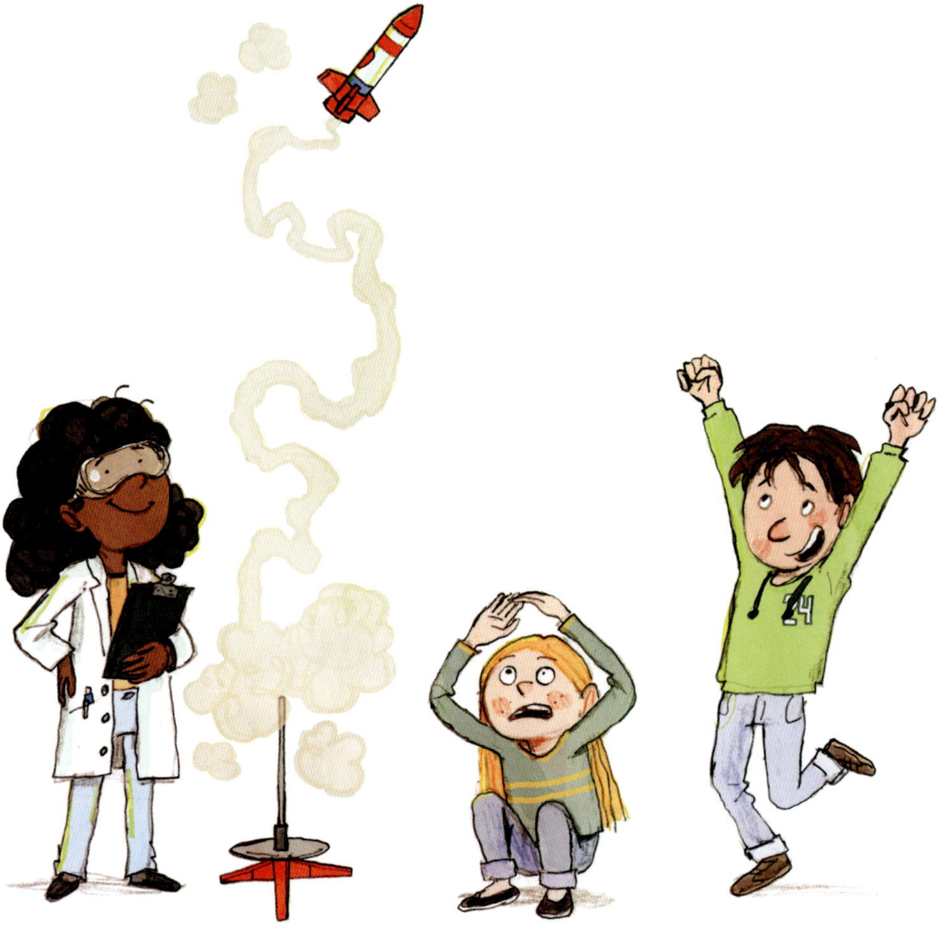

#7 Study halls when you can get your homework done

#8 ...or doodle your name in your notebook a hundred times with gel pens.

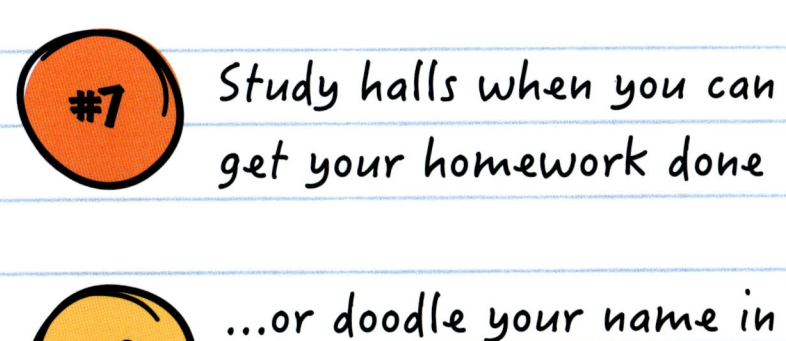

 A much bigger, cooler gym.

 Next-level gym equipment (like a climbing wall and a regulation hoop).

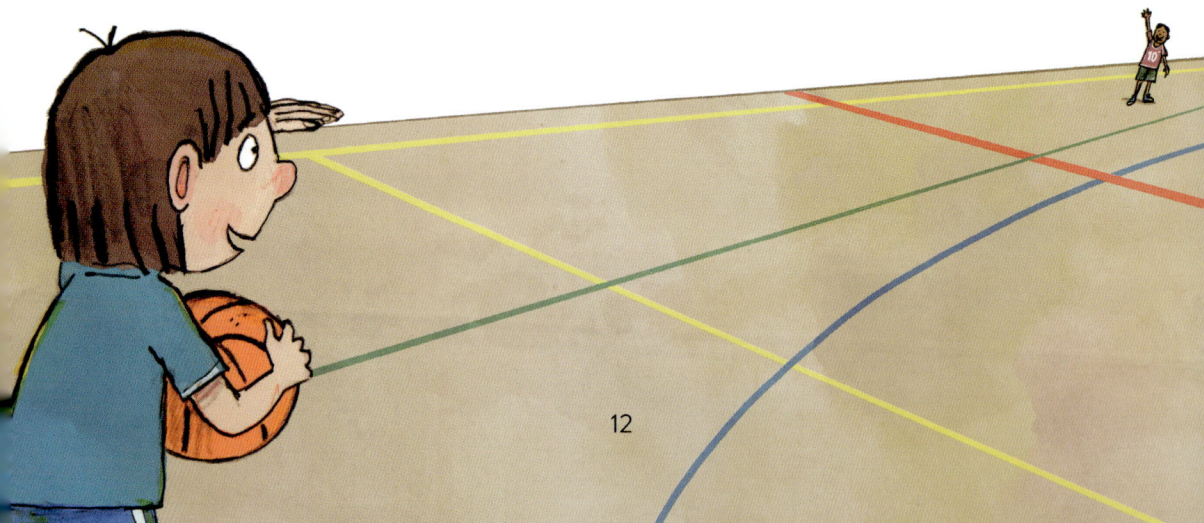

 A library you can hang out in after school.

 So many books, you could swim in them!

 An earlier release time. Seize the day, people!

 Way more guy teachers. Let's face it: They were kind of an endangered species in elementary school.

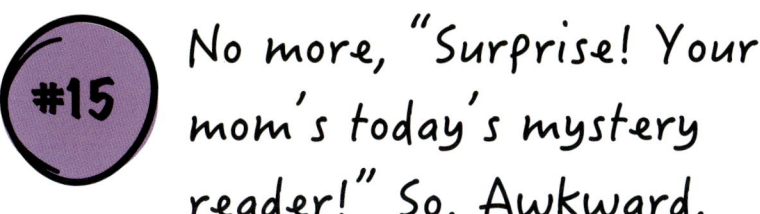

#15 No more, "Surprise! Your mom's today's mystery reader!" So. Awkward.

#16 Rolling into school on your bike or scooter!

 Drama club.

 Language classes. In case you want to be an international person of mystery.

 A new name in a foreign language.

Hola. ¡Me llamo Gustavo!

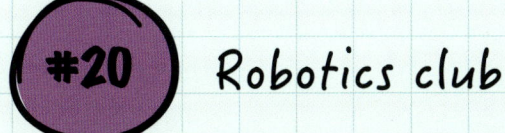 Robotics club.

 Make-your-own-club club. Don't see a group you fit into? Start your own!

 Homeroom: where you can finish waking up.

 Morning announcements read by ~~teachers~~ kids!

 A schedule that lets you switch rooms before you get bored.

 A little space from the kids who drove you nuts in elementary school.

 Chairs that aren't attached to desks. Can we all admit how weird those were?

 Lab equipment like beakers, test tubes, flasks, and pipettes (little squeeze-y things)!

#28 Controlled fire brought to you by...the Bunsen burner.

#29 Chemicals that smoke, bubble, and stink. In the best way.

#30 Dissection...if you dare!

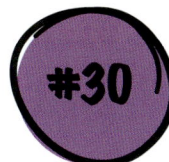

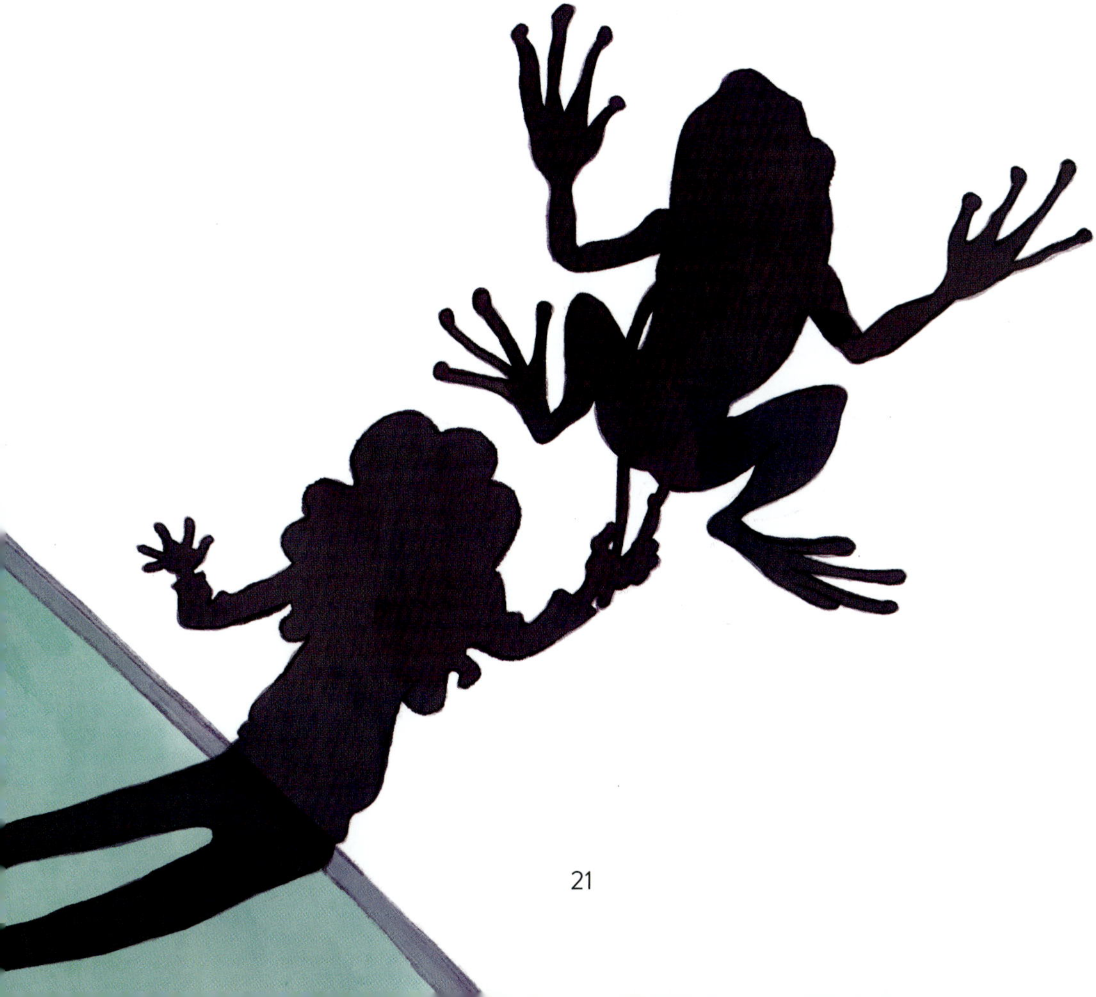

 An emotional support dog. (Ours is still being trained, but we love him.)

#32 Fast new computers with (audible gasp) online access.

 Kids with more style, personality, and attitude.

 Class discussions where you can actually disagree and say what you REALLY think.

#35 Instruments you start off being horrible at, then become awesome at!

#36 Snack breaks while you work or study.

 The joy of sitting wherever you want in the lunchroom.

 Bigger, cooler food options!

 Dreamy school supplies with extra features. I'm talking about binders with pockets, maps, dividers, and tabs!

 Actual grades, so you can finally get that A+ and brag about it.

 Better art supplies.

 X-ACTO knives: where art and danger meet.

#43 Geography competitions.

#44 Spelling bees.

#45 Holiday parties and international parties and perfect attendance parties and everyone-passed-the-test parties.

 **#46** Cooler field trips. Here we go, famous sites, adventure courses, and foreign countries!

 **#47** Meeting kids who could be your FUTURE BEST FRIENDS.

 School sports teams

 ...and a mascot to get you hyped up.

 Encouraging coaches.

 Guidance counselors you can stop by and see whenever.

#52

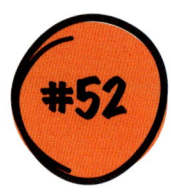

Crushes and first loves and break-ups and get-back-togethers.
How can you NOT love the drama?

#53

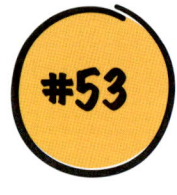

Middle school dances.
Legendary good times.

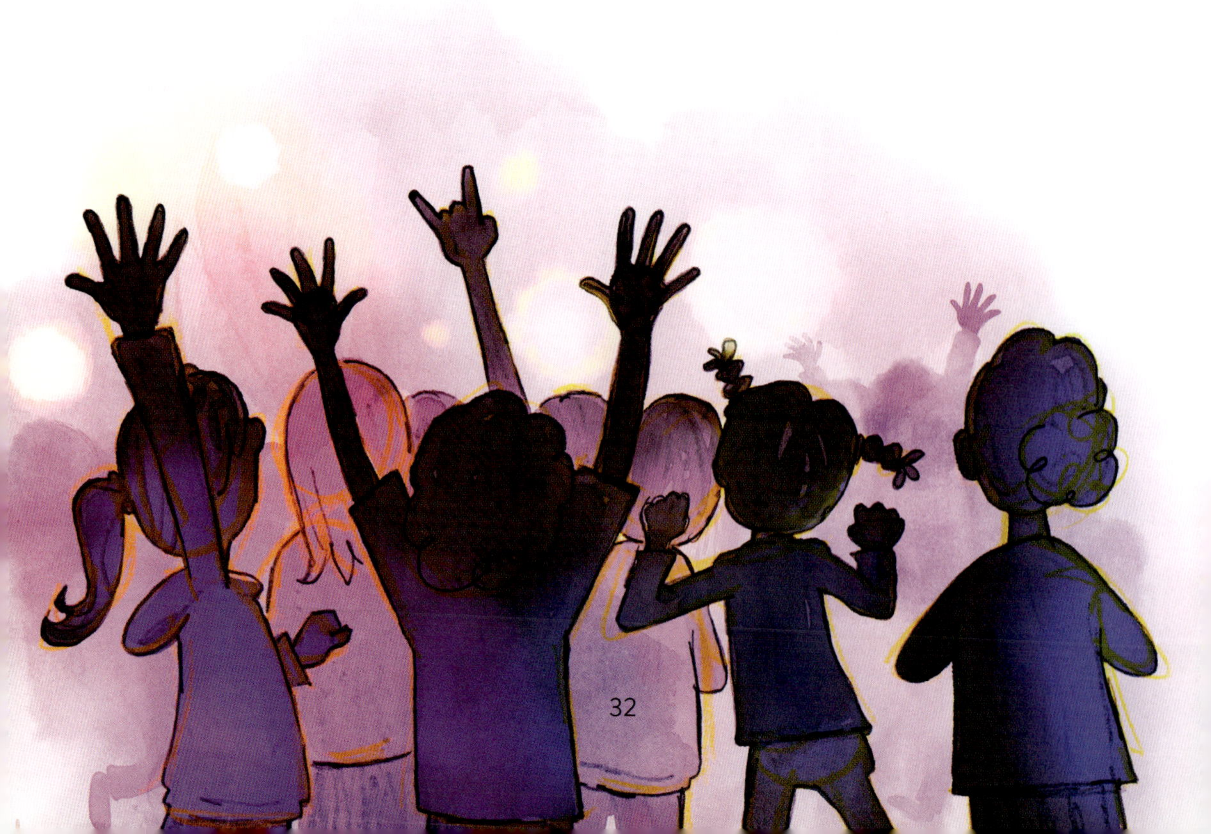

 Passing notes in class without getting caught. Total. Adrenaline. Rush.

 A later bedtime (if you can clear it with management).

 New spaces where you can chill or study or daydream.

 Group projects with friends.

 **#58** Teachers you ALMOST enjoy hanging out with.

 **#59** Sleepover parties, laser tag parties, and escape room parties on the weekends.

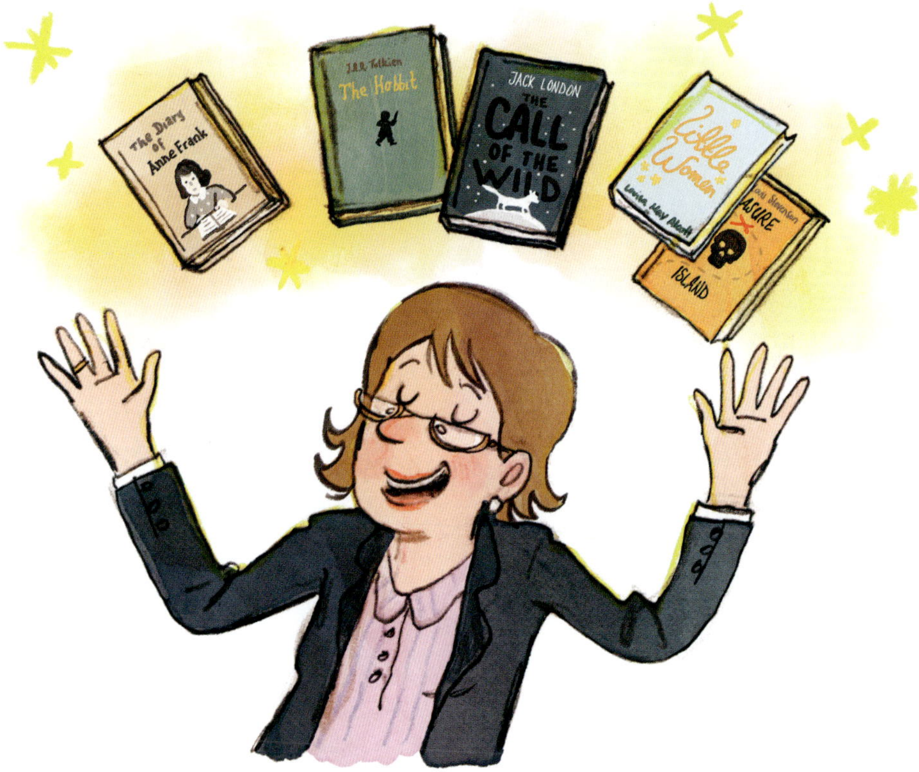

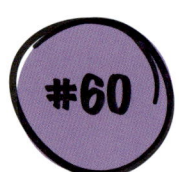

#60 World-famous books in English class.

#61 Talking about real world stuff in social studies.

 Putting on plays...with cool props!

 Getting to sing newer, better songs in chorus.

 #64 Your very own school newspaper.

#65 A chance to run for president! (of student council, that is)

 Pep rallies where you can yell as loud as you want.

 Spirit week.

 Your own phone! (Or at least the promise of one in the future. #goals #akidcandream.)

 Teachers who totally love their tech.

 A computer lab with cool gadgets (like a virtual reality headset or a 3D printer)!

 A garden or greenhouse where you can vibe out with nature.

 Big-brained activities like math club

 ...chess club

 ...and academic team competitions.

#75 Movies on the last day before holiday vacations!

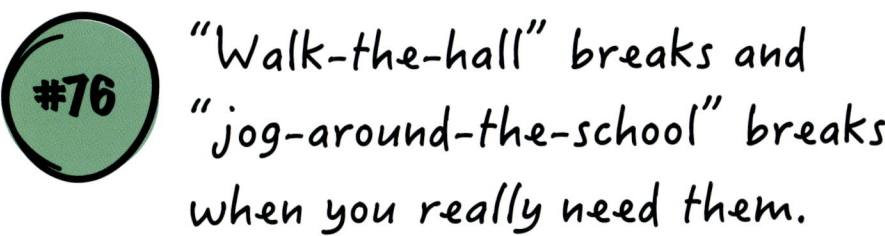
#76 "Walk-the-hall" breaks and "jog-around-the-school" breaks when you really need them.

 Classes that teach you real life skills, like how to buy stocks

 ...how to type faster

 ...how to eat right

 ...how to sew up a hole in your sock

 ...and how to build a bird house. (Next time, you'll design it so the bird can fit inside.)

 Bigger, cooler athletic fields.

 A chance to try a new sport...

 or get better at an old one.

#85 Talent shows.

#86 Middle school pride.

 A chance to cheer for your friends at plays

 ...games

 ...concerts

 ...and musicals.

 Electives like Board Game Design, Photography, and Creative Writing.

 Classroom v classroom showdowns.

 Being around older kids instead of younger ones.

 Seeing your big brother or your friend's big sister in the hallways. MAJOR STREET CRED.

 Braces and growth spurts are totally normal here.

 Trying out new looks is a thing.

 Even your locker can be stylish. Think disco balls, mirrors, stickers, and posters.

 English teachers who let you journal ALL your feelings.

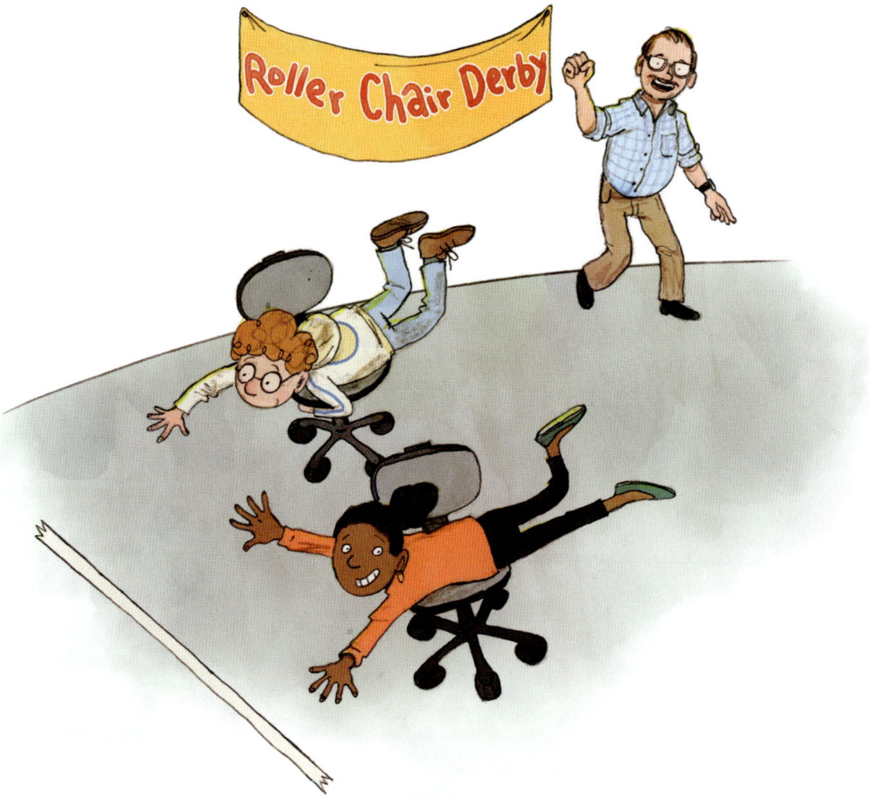

#99 Rolling chairs. They're basically skateboards with seats.

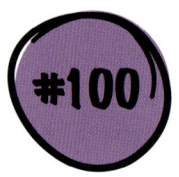

#100 Teachers who act more like your cool aunts and uncles than your parents.

 A chance to learn coding and become an absolute cyber-genius.

 Stickers and candy ~~bribes~~ rewards from teachers when you do your homework, or stay quiet for more than, like, five seconds.

 Goodbye, before- and after-school care. Hello independence.

 More classroom pets, like turtles, frogs, fish, and pet rocks.

 Board games, fidgets, and free time when you finish something early.

 Teacher jokes that are so bad they're funny.

 #107 Two words that'll save your grade (and your butt): Extra. Credit.

 #108 No more awkward play dates set up by moms. Who you hang out with is up to YOU.

 #109 Art class where you get to be as weird as you want.

 #110 Plenty of chances to show your bravery and stand up for others.

 #111 Better, cooler projects, like recording a podcast or making a video.

 Hallway partner work. It's almost like the teachers trust you to be out there unsupervised!

 Trading your pencil in for a pen. There's a whole world of writing utensils out there you haven't been allowed to use.

 Dodge ball. Love it or hate it, that game gets the heart pumping.

 Class clowns who make you laugh so hard you snort.

 The dream of making honor roll.

 Earning no-homework passes.

 Yearbooks that capture the whole wild and crazy experience.
(Real ones that aren't just papers stapled together.)

 Learning to love yourself, even when you feel a little awkward.
(It might help to know that your parents looked like this in middle school. And they got this far!)

 Visiting your old school and feeling like a total hero.

 Change.
It might freak you out at first, but life is an adventure.